Clowning Around

by Tracey West

Illustrated by Gregg Schigiel

SCHOLASTIC INC.

New York   Toronto   London   Auckland   Sydney
Mexico City   New Delhi   Hong Kong   Buenos Aires

Published by Scholastic Inc.,
90 Old Sherman Turnpike, Danbury, Connecticut 06816.

SCHOLASTIC and associated logos are trademarks
and/or registered trademarks of Scholastic Inc.

ISBN 0-439-56300-3

First Scholastic Printing, May 2004

Chapters

Chapter 1

A Krabby Patty Disaster

SpongeBob SquarePants loved working at the Krusty Krab. His passion for making Krabby Patties was legendary.

SpongeBob gazed at his newest Krabby Patty with love. "Farewell, friend," he said. "I can't keep your perfect steamy goodness to myself!"

SpongeBob pushed the Krabby Patty through the order window. He picked up his spatula and got ready to flip another batch of patties.

SpongeBob froze. Something was wrong
a Krabby Patty? It couldn't be!
SpongeBob rushed into the dining room.
customer was examining his Krabby
atty with a ruler. Mr. Krabs was anxiously

Then he heard a yell.

"There is something wrong wit

Krabby Patty!"

looking over the customer's shoulder.

"This Krabby Patty is a mess!" complained the cranky customer. "This piece of lettuce is one-sixteenth of an inch too long. I can't eat lettuce that is too long!"

"That's ridiculous," said SpongeBob. "My Krabby Patties are always perfect!"

"See for yourself," sneered the customer.

SpongeBob bent down to examine the patty. The cranky customer was right.

Horror filled every nook and cranny of SpongeBob's spongy body.

Tears welled up in SpongeBob's eyes.
"Making Krabby Patties is what I do
best," he said. "If I can't do it perfectly, then
I shouldn't do it at all!"

SpongeBob shoved his hat and spatula into the claws of a stunned Mr. Krabs.

"Good-bye, Mr. Krabs," he said sadly. "I don't deserve to make Krabby Patties anymore."

Chapter 2
Send in the Clownfish

SpongeBob sat at the bus stop. He didn't know where he was going. He just knew he couldn't go back to the Krusty Krab.

"Life is meaningless if I can't make Krabby Patties," SpongeBob sobbed. "I don't know how to do anything else!"

Then he heard the rumble of a bus.

But it wasn't the Bikini Bottom bus. It was a circus bus! Three colorful clownfish tumbled out of the door.

"We saw you crying," said one. "Clownfish hate to see someone cry. Don't be such a sad sponge.

Cheer up!"

"I can't cheer up," SpongeBob said glumly. "My life has no meaning. I thought I was born to make the world's best Krabby Patties, but I'm just not good enough. I'll never be good at anything!"

The clownfish looked at each other. "My name's Al," said one, "and this here is Slim and Shorty. Why don't you come with us? Maybe we can find you something to do at the circus."

SpongeBob thought and thought about it. "I can't make people happy with my Krabby Patties anymore," he said finally. "But the circus makes people happy. Maybe joining the circus isn't such a bad idea."

"That's the spirit!" said Al.

SpongeBob gave the Krusty Krab one last look.

"Good-bye forever, my wonderful patties," he said softly. Then he boarded the bus.

Chapter 3
Krusty Customers

Back at the Krusty Krab, orders were piling up. Mr. Krabs was getting desperate.

"Please, darlin'," Mr. Krabs pleaded with his daughter, Pearl. "It's just 'til I find SpongeBob and bring him back. Won't you help out your dear old dad?"

"Do I have to, Daddy?" Pearl whined. "I just got a facial, and it's so greasy back here!"

Mr. Krabs searched all over Bikini Bottom for SpongeBob. "I can't let a day go by without my best fry cook," he said. But there was no trace of the yellow fellow.

Finally, Mr. Krabs returned to the
restaurant. "I can't find SpongeBob
anywhere!" he moaned. "This is terrible!"

"Oh, yes," Squidward said in a bored voice.
"Just terrible."

Mr. Krabs had to do
something. Nobody
could make Krabby
Patties like SpongeBob.

A look of
determination filled
his beady eyes.

"I will find you,
SpongeBob
SquarePants," he
vowed. "I will find you,
no matter what it takes!"

Chapter 4
Try, Try Again

Meanwhile, at the circus tent,
SpongeBob was contemplating a new life.
"All I know how to do is flip Krabby
Patties," he told his new friends. "What

kind of job can I do in the circus?"

"Don't worry," Al said. "We'll find a job for you. But we've got to hurry. It's almost time for the circus to start!"

"Maybe we can shoot him out of a cannon," Slim said.

Al, Slim, and Shorty pushed and shoved with all their might, but SpongeBob didn't fit into the cannon.

"Well, you know what they say,"
SpongeBob said. "You can't fit a square
sponge into a round hole!"

"Maybe he can walk the tightrope," said Shorty.

SpongeBob tried. But his square body was too big and his legs were too short. He just couldn't keep his balance.

"It's no use!" SpongeBob said sadly. "I'm no good at anything!"

SpongeBob started to sob again. "I give up. I might as well leave!"

With tears filling his eyes, he stumbled blindly toward the exit. But as he neared the doorway, he slipped on some juggling balls . . . did a backflip . . . and landed face first in a cream pie!

"That was brilliant!" Slim cried.

"Hilarious!" laughed Shorty.

"Perfect!" Al said. "You can join our clown act."

"There's no time to practice," Al said. "We need to get you into your costume!" The clownfish gave SpongeBob a red nose and a clown costume of his very own.

"See?" said Al. "You fit right in!"

SpongeBob gazed at his reflection in the mirror. "Maybe I can do it," he said. "I'll be the clowniest SpongeClown ever!"

Chapter 5
Big Show under the Big Top

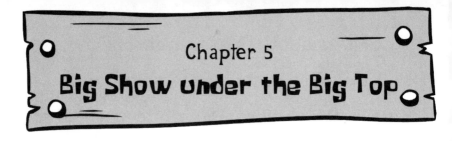

Everyone in Bikini Bottom came to the circus.

Mr. Krabs came to search for SpongeBob. "This is the only place I haven't looked," Mr. Krabs said sadly to himself. He gazed at the spatula in his claw. "If I ever

find SpongeBob, I hope this spatula will remind him of how happy he was at the Krusty Krab. Oh, how me boy loved flipping Krabby Patties!"

The lights dimmed and the show began. The high-wire artists flew through the air. The trained lionfish and the swordfish swallower wowed the crowd.

Finally, it was time for the clownfish act, but SpongeBob was nervous.

"What if I can't do it?" he asked the other clowns.

"Just have fun, SpongeBob," Al responded, pushing him toward the ring. "That's what clowns do."

"I'll do my best," SpongeBob vowed.
He ran out and threw a pie at Slim. He
squirted water at Shorty. It felt great to try
something new!

"I'm doing it!" SpongeBob said happily.
"Maybe I'm good at
something after all!"

Up in the stands, Mr. Krabs couldn't believe his eyes. "Is that SpongeBob?" he asked in disbelief. "Why that boy is a born entertainer!"

Mr. Krabs looked down at the spatula clutched in his claw. "I guess I'm too late," he muttered. "It looks like SpongeBob has found his true calling." He slowly stood and walked toward the exit, tossing the spatula over his shoulder.

Down in the ring, Al threw a bunch of balls into the air. The three clownfish juggled the balls skillfully, as the crowd cheered and whistled.

Then, without warning, Al tossed the balls to SpongeBob.

"Your turn, SpongeBob!" Al yelled.

SpongeBob froze. Juggle? He couldn't juggle. A wave of panic washed over him.

Time slowed to a crawl as SpongeBob braced himself for another failure. Then, out of the corner of his eye, SpongeBob noticed a familiar object sailing toward him.

"My spatula!" he said wonderingly. "How did you get here?" And then, in a flash, SpongeBob knew what to do. "Just imagine that each ball is a delicious Krabby Patty," he told himself. "You can do it, SpongeBob!"

With lightning speed,
SpongeBob caught the spatula
and began to flip the balls,
one after the other.
"I'm doing it! I'm juggling!"
he thought proudly.
  It was a beautiful sight!
The crowd went wild.

When the circus was over, the clownfish gathered around SpongeBob.

"You're a great clown, SpongeBob," Al said.

"But he's an even better fry cook," said a familiar voice.

Mr. Krabs ran up. "I couldn't leave without talking to you, SpongeBob. I need you at the Krusty Krab," he said. "Nobody makes Krabby Patties like you do. Please come back to me, laddy!"

SpongeBob looked at his spatula. Then he looked at his new friends. "You're right, Mr. Krabs," he finally said. "Let's all go to the Krusty Krab!"

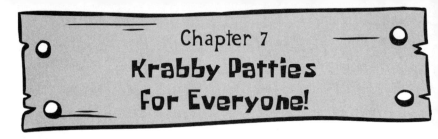

Pearl was very relieved to see SpongeBob back in his place at the stove. "Thank goodness," she said. "This greasy kitchen is no place for a delicate girl like me."

SpongeBob got right to work and made Krabby Patties for everyone.

"It's good to be back, my mouth-watering mounds of fabulous flavor," SpongeBob lovingly told a plate of patties. "I promise never to leave you again!"

Then someone yelled out, "There is something wrong with my Krabby Patty!"

It was the same cranky customer who didn't like his Krabby Patty before. He had his ruler out again.

"This bun is too small," he said. "It should be—"

SPLAT! Al hit him with a pie in the face.

SPLASH! Shorty squirted him with water.

"Thanks, guys!" SpongeBob said.

"We're clowns," Al said, shrugging. "That's what we do best."

SpongeBob smiled. "And I make

Krabby Patties," he said. "That's what I do best. Right, Mr. Krabs?"

"Right!" said Mr. Krabs. "Now stop clowning around and get back to work!"